Based on the TV series *CatDog*®
Created by Peter Hannan as seen on NICKELODEON®

Editorial Consultants: Peter Hannan and Robert Lamoreaux
Additional assistance provided by the CatDog Production Team.

SIMON SPOTLIGHT
An imprint of Simon & Schuster
Children's Publishing Division
1230 Avenue of the Americas
New York, NY 10020

Produced by Bumpy Slide Books
Designed by sheena needham•ess design and development

Manufactured in the United States of America

Additional material was originally published in *CatDog Joke Book* and
CatDog Trivia Book, Copyright © Simon Spotlight/Nickelodeon.

This edition published by Grolier Books.
Grolier Books is a division of Grolier Enterprises, Inc.

ISBN 0-7172-8915-X

CatDog Catcher

by K. Emily Hutta and Eliot Brown
illustrated by Emilie Kong

Simon Spotlight/Nickelodeon

Dog had a bad case of spring fever. "It's springtime! I wanna sniff, I wanna dig, I wanna run!" he panted. "What do you feel like doing first, Cat?"

"I feel like lying right here with the sun on my belly," Cat answered. "This is purr-fect!"

"I know something even better to do!"
Dog said. "Let's go mark some territory!"
"Ow! My body, my body!" Cat wailed.

"Stop, Dog, stop!" shouted Cat.
"We're on Greaser turf now!"

But it was too late. The Greasers had spotted them.

Just as Cliff, Shriek, and Lube caught up with CatDog—SWAT—an enormous net trapped them all!

"Leaping Lumbago!" cried Rancid
Rabbit, the dogcatcher. "Four dogs for
the price of one!"

"Make that three dumb dogs and
one angry cat," Cat said.

"What, what, what?!?" Rancid Rabbit asked. He pulled Cat out of the net. "Get lost. I have no bones to pick with any cats today."

Cat was not happy. "Don't let it happen again," he said.

Then Rancid Rabbit emptied his net into the back of his truck. He sped off toward the city pound.

Dog kept his face hidden until the coast was clear. "Close call," he said. "Thanks, Cat."

Back at home, Dog tried to sit still. He sniffed the air. "Cat, do you smell spring in the air?" he asked. "I think I smell the scent of whitefish chub."

Cat's mouth started to water.
"White . . . fish . . . chub?" he replied.
His eyes were widening. "What are we
waiting for?"

CatDog raced over the hill and into town. Suddenly they spotted the dogcatcher's truck.

Cat pulled Dog behind a fence. "Over here! Quick!" Cat said. "We have to keep all four of our eyes wide open."

Dog stuck his head around the corner to see if the coast was clear. SWAT! Once again, CatDog was trapped in the dogcatcher's net.

"Ah-ha!" Rancid Rabbit shouted.

Surprise! Rancid Rabbit couldn't believe his eyes. Cat was back in his net! He didn't know that Cat had switched places with Dog again.

"Well, well, well," Cat said. "Rancid, I think you're a few carrots shy of a bunch!"

"Yeah, you crazy rabbit guy!" Dog exclaimed.

Oh no! CatDog's cover was blown!

In no time at all, Dog was cooling his paws in the POUND!

Cat was very upset. "This is just terrific!" he complained.

"Sorry, Cat," said Dog.

Next, Cat called Randolph from a phone booth for help. Inside the cell, the Greasers surrounded Dog.

"Now you're gonna get it," Cliff said.

"Can't run now," Lube said. "Uh, at least not too far."

"Wait!" Shriek shouted. "Does anyone notice something different here?"

The other Greasers and Dog all shook their heads no.

"Cat's not here!" Shriek exclaimed.

Cliff gave Dog a big smile. "Welcome to the gang, Dog!" he said.

Dog looked uncertain. "But what about Cat?" he asked.

"Forget about him," Shriek said.

"Yeah," said Cliff. "Us jaildogs gotta stick together."

"Uh, okay," agreed Dog.

Cat was still on the phone. "Okay, Randolph. You sure you can pull this off?"

"No problem," replied Randolph. "It'll be a piece of cake!"

Back in the cell, Cliff told Dog the Greasers' plan. "We're bustin' out. And since you are new to our gang, you have to dig our escape tunnel."

Dog didn't know what to say. "Thanks, guys. I won't let you down."

"You'd better not!" replied Cliff. "Here's your spoon. Now, dig!"

Dog worked hard at digging. Dog also worked hard at eating. The worms and dirt looked too good to resist.

While Dog stuffed his face, Cat decided to take action. Cat slipped into Dog's cell.

"Hiya, Cat," said Dog. "Where have you been?"

"I've been trying to get us out of here," said Cat.

Just then Randolph came down the hall. "I am from the law firm of Hairball, Hairball, Kitty, and Litter," he told Rancid Rabbit. "My client says that you are a cat burglar!"

"Your client?" Rancid Rabbit asked. He turned and saw Cat inside the cell.

Randolph explained: "My client is a cat. Not a dog!"

"Huh?" said Rancid Rabbit.

"This is a DOG pound," said Randolph. "You have jailed a CatDog. Half of this animal shouldn't be here at all. You must release them both at once!"

"Hey! What about us?" Cliff shouted. "We're your jailhouse buddies, Dog!"

"I'm not a jailhouse dog anymore," replied Dog.

"This ain't the end," Cliff called. "You're going to get it. Just wait until we get out of here!"

Back at home, Dog asked, "What do you feel like doing now?"

"I'm happy right here," Cat said.

"Wanna go mark some territory?" asked Dog.

"This *is* our territory," replied Cat.

And that's exactly where they both wanted to be.

All About Cat

Family history: Traces ancestry to the royal cats of ancient Egypt

Favorite food: Whitefish chub, sushi, and whitefish pudding

Favorite activities: Lying in the sun, listening to opera and classical polka, and trying to mingle with the upper classes of Nearburg

Favorite book: 1001 Uses for Hairballs

Favorite Greaser: None!

Favorite TV show: Battle of the Opera Wrestling Star

Best friends: Dog, Lola, Mervis, and Dunglap

Least favorite food: Garbage

Hobbies: Cooking and writing his deepest thoughts in his diary

Least favorite activity: Getting beat up by the Greasers

Favorite swimsuit: A waterproof one

Secret crush: Shriek

Favorite water sport: None!

Most prized possessions:
Mr. Loofah, big yarn ball, and scratching post

Biggest wish:
To get rich quick

All About Dog

Best friends: Cat, Winslow, Lola, Mervis, and Dunglap

Family restaurant: Taco Depot

Favorite food: Tacos, tacos, tacos! Garbage, garbage, garbage!

Favorite activities:

Chasing garbage trucks, mailmen, squirrels, and paper boys; mud wrestling; and playing fetch

Least favorite activity:	Sitting still
Favorite action figure:	Mean Bob
Pet peeve:	When another dog uses his favorite fire hydrant
Favorite movie:	*Mean Bob in Space Part 12*
Favorite book:	*Squidman, The Aliens That Moved in Next-Door and Sucked Brains,* and all other comic books
Favorite dance:	The Cha-cha
Most afraid of:	Toothpickhead
Secret alter-ego:	Dog the Mighty, a superhero
Secret admirer:	Shriek
Most prized possessions:	His bone collection hidden in a bone cellar; and a lamb chop from 1987, which he hides under the refrigerator
Biggest wish:	To own the biggest bone in the world

Joke Break

What does Cat call it when he burps up a taco?
Dog's lunch.

What do you get if you cross a hungry cat and a canary?
A cat who isn't hungry anymore.

Why did cat cross the road?
Because Dog was chasing a squirrel.

What do cats and dogs have in common?
The letter "s."

What are Lube's clothes made of?
Mutt-terial.

What does Dog have in common with a tree?
They both have barks.

How does Dog spell paradise?
G-A-R-B-A-G-E T-R-U-C-K

What's worse than raining cats and dogs?
Hailing elephants.

What is Winslow's favorite cereal?
Cream of wit.

How does Dog like to travel?
On a mutt-a-cycle.

CatDog's Rules to Live By

Decide who's going to lead before you get on the dance floor.

Don't go anywhere without your brother (not that you have a choice).

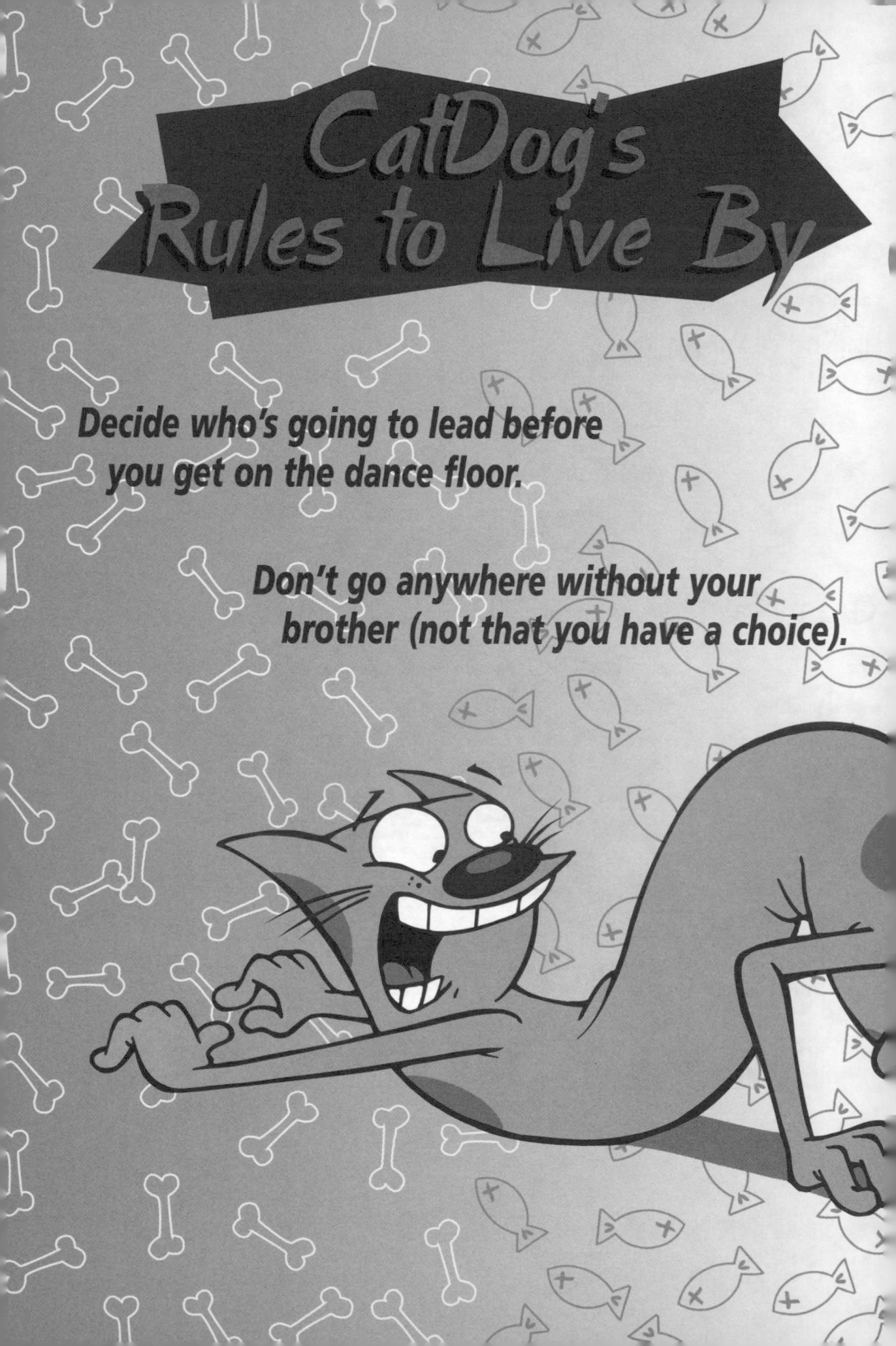

Always take cover when Dog eats spicy tacos.
The results can be explosive—for Cat.

Steer clear of "all you can eat" places.
They are dangerous, especially for Cat,
who shares a stomach with Dog!

Don't mess with the Greasers,
or you'll end up in a knot.

Never trust a Greaser.

Test your CatDog IQ!

Think you're a CatDog trivia whiz?
Then give this test your best shot!

1. Who is older–Cat or Dog?
   a) Cat
   b) Dog
   c) they're the same age

2. Who does Winslow like better?
   a) Dog
   b) Cat
   c) himself

3. Who does Shriek have a crush on?
   a) Cliff
   b) Dog
   c) Randolph

4. What animal was once accidentally glued to Cliff's back?
   a) a pig
   b) a squirrel
   c) a squid

5. What musical show does Cat try out for in "All About CatDog"?
   a) Abe Lincoln: Superstar!
   b) Katz!
   c) The Very Hungry CatDog

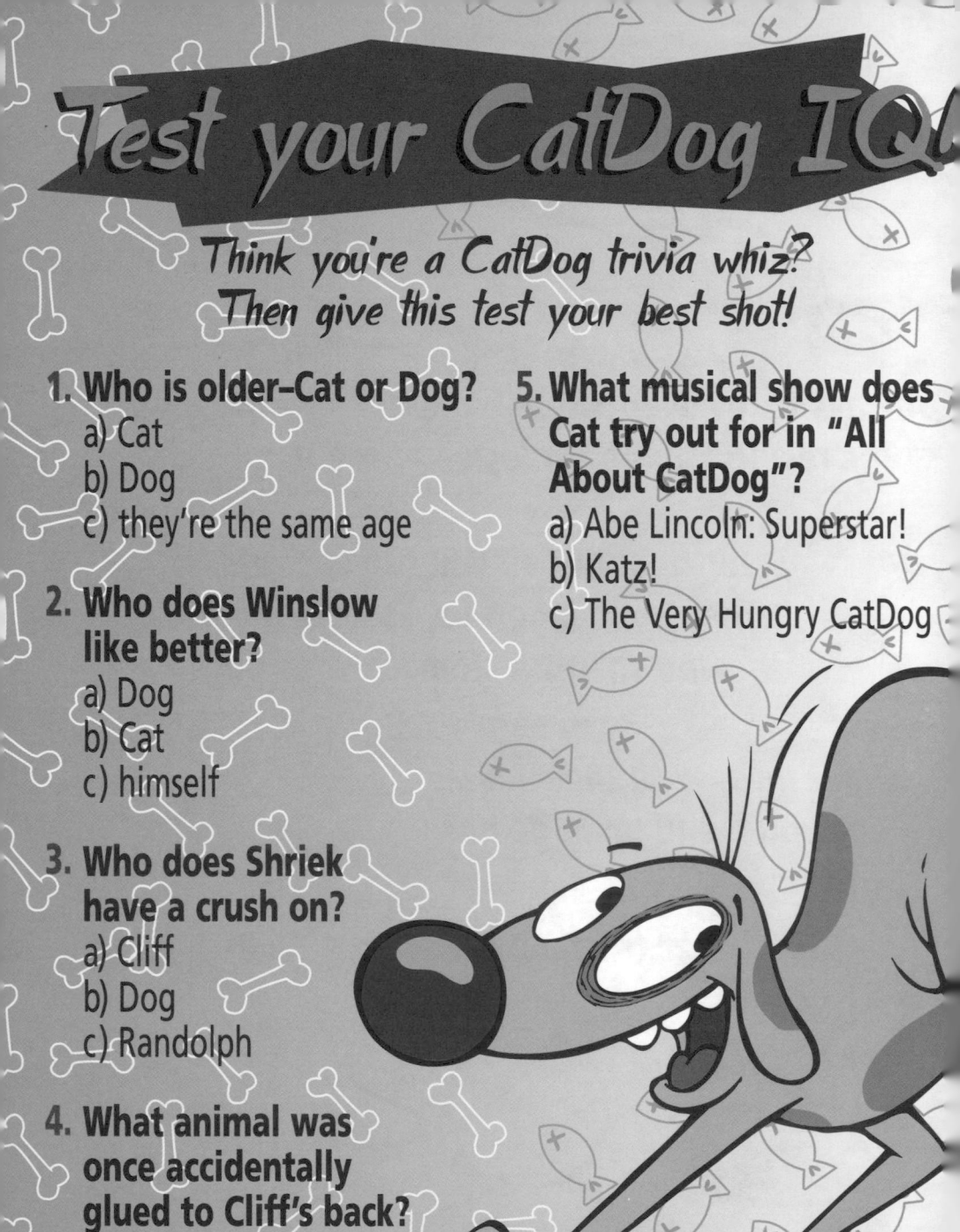

6. In "CatDog's End," how many transplants has Randolph had?
   a) 94
   b) 6
   c) 13

7. In "CatDog Food," what are the products Rancid Rabbit wants CatDog to promote?
   a) a television, a hammock, and a ukulele
   b) a hotel towel, a brick, and a bus pass
   c) a dog bowl, a light bulb, and a fish tank

8. In "The Collector," when Cat is collecting Mean Bob action figures, what new action figure becomes more popular?
   a) Evil Eric
   b) Annoying Adam
   c) Wicked Wally

9. When Winslow catches Cat reading Dog's diary, what happens?
   a) Winslow tells Dog
   b) Winslow makes Cat his servant
   c) Winslow reads it too

10. In the episode "Pumped," what does Dog drink that makes him so muscular?
   a) Choco-kraut
   b) Choco-muscle
   c) goat's milk

ANSWERS:
1) a
2) a or c
3) b
4) b
5) a
6) c
7) b
8) a
9) b
10) b